Groundwood Books / House of Anansi Press
groundwoodbooks.com

We gratefully acknowledge for their financial support of our publishing program
the Canada Council for the Arts, the Ontario Arts Council and the Government
of Canada.

  Canada Council   Conseil des Arts
for the Arts   du Canada

ONTARIO ARTS COUNCIL
CONSEIL DES ARTS DE L'ONTARIO
an Ontario government agency
un organisme du gouvernement de l'Ontario

With the participation of the Government of Canada   Canadä
Avec la participation du gouvernement du Canada

Library and Archives Canada Cataloguing in Publication
Title: Nice try, Charlie! / Matt James.
Names: James, Matt, author, illustrator.
Identifiers: Canadiana (print) 20190230177 | Canadiana (ebook) 20190231009
| ISBN 9781773061801 (hardcover) | ISBN 9781773061818 (EPUB) | ISBN
9781773063539 (Kindle)
Classification: LCC PS8619.A6357 N53 2020 | DDC jC813/.6—dc23

The illustrations were done in acrylic, gouache and ink on masonite.
Dimensional elements were made using cut paper, photographs, cardboard,
masking tape and scroll-sawn masonite, all painted with acrylic. A few
illustrations have elements that were done with an iPad.

Design by Michael Solomon
Printed and bound in China

NICE TRY, CHARLIE!

Matt James

GROUNDWOOD BOOKS
HOUSE OF ANANSI PRESS
TORONTO   BERKELEY

For Rebecca, Noble
and Julius

Charlie finds things.

And he finds things to do with the things that he finds. Sometimes he finds it harder than he'd like to admit, but he tries.

There really is an
amazing amount
of garbage lying
around.

It is even up in
the trees.

And so is
Aunt Myrtle's cat.

Charlie gets him
down, being
careful not to
get scratched.

And then Charlie notices his friend Steve sitting on the stairs.

But Steve only sighs.
Steve has a lot on his mind. Also he is pie-eyed.
And by that I mean he eyes a pie.

Aunt Myrtle spots it, too.

"What is it?"
Aunt Myrtle yells.

"It's a huge tart!" Charlie says.

In fact, it is a pie.

Charlie's heart stirs. "We should eat this right now!" he proclaims, not believing his good fortune.

"Not so fast!" Aunt Myrtle yells.
Aunt Myrtle always yells.

Charlie looks up at her with
raised eyebrows.

Aunt Myrtle looks down and
yells again, "Does that pie
belong to you?"

And so Charlie closes up
the box and sets off to find
the owner.

Margaret's ball has gone over the fence. Charlie tries to throw it back to her.

Then he tries again ...

and he tries again after that.

By the way, are you missing a pie?

And then Margaret goes and
gets the ball herself.

Over by the park, Charlie can hear an awful racket. Malcolm is playing his tuba.

Charlie can't imagine that it is supposed to sound this way, but Malcolm doesn't want any of Charlie's help. Also, it isn't Malcolm's pie.

A little while later, Charlie happens upon a tire.

The birds are tired.
And it isn't their pie, either.

No one Charlie talks to is missing a pie, it seems.

Charlie walks back to where
Steve was sitting.

Steve sits there still.
"Are you okay?" Charlie asks him.

"I don't know," says Steve.
They are both feeling kind of sad.
"Yeah," says Charlie. "It's hard to know."

Steve hands Charlie his binoculars and suggests he look through them backwards. It makes everything smaller, but Charlie still feels more or less the same. And they are both getting hungry.

And so is this dog.

Meanwhile, Aunt Myrtle knows just what to do. She gets into her elevator, rides it down and calls everyone together.

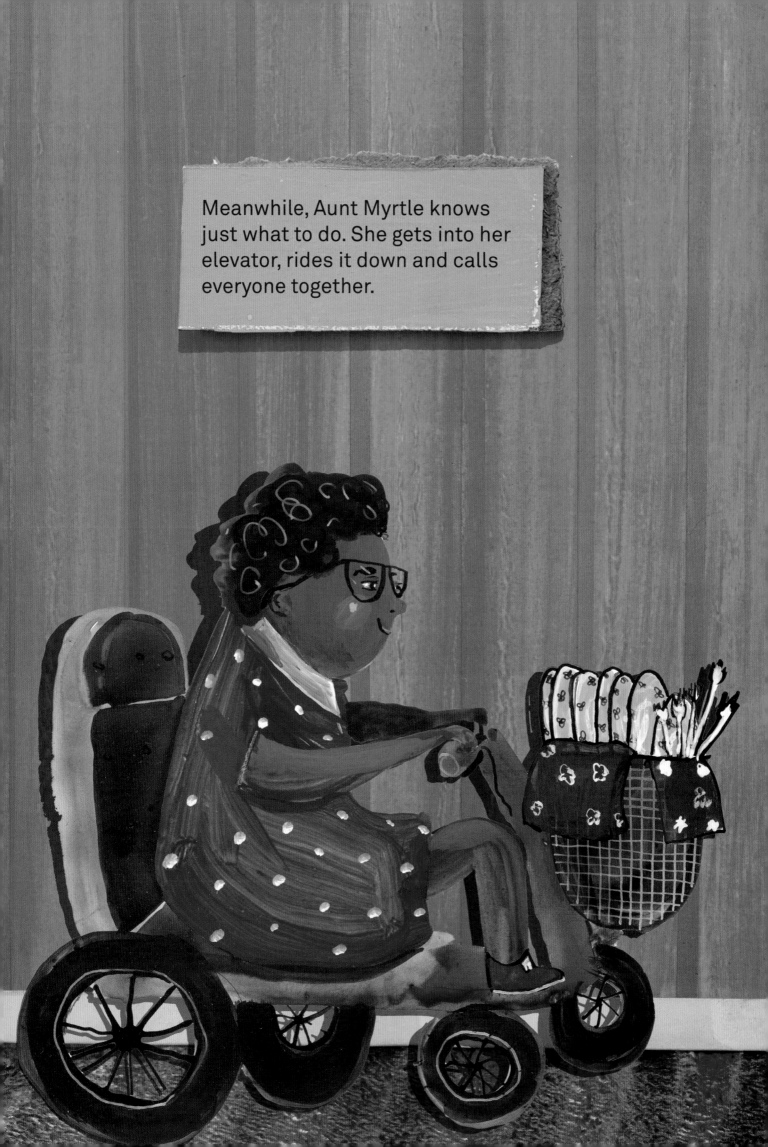

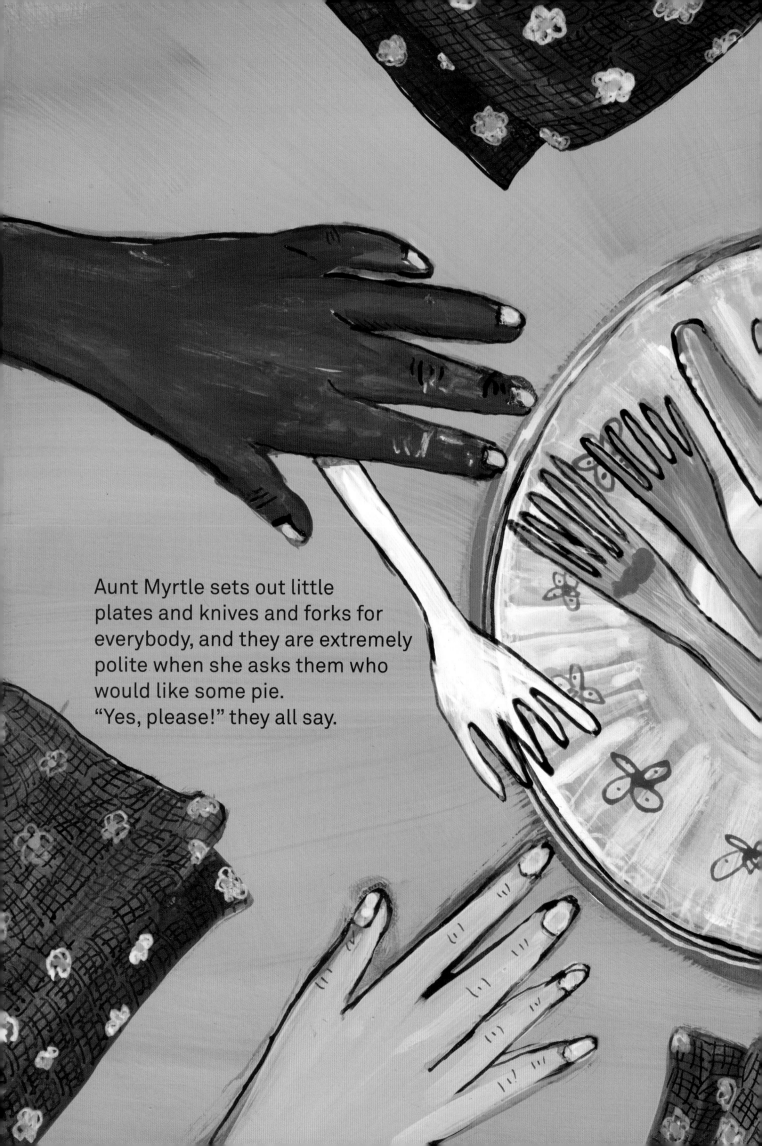

Aunt Myrtle sets out little plates and knives and forks for everybody, and they are extremely polite when she asks them who would like some pie.
"Yes, please!" they all say.

Charlie finds things.
And he finds things to do with the things
that he finds.

He never did find out whose pie it was,
but at least he tried.

THE
END